VIKING

Published by Penguin Group

Penguin Young Readers Group, 345 Hudson Street, New York, New York 10014, U.S.A.

Penguin Group (Canada), 90 Eglinton Avenue East, Suite 700, Toronto, Ontario, Canada M4P 2Y3
(a division of Pearson Penguin Canada Inc.)

Penguin Books Ltd, 80 Strand, London WC2R 0RL, England

Penguin Ireland, 25 St Stephen's Green, Dublin 2, Ireland (a division of Penguin Books Ltd)

Penguin Group (Australia), 250 Camberwell Road, Camberwell, Victoria 3124, Australia (a division of
Pearson Australia Group Pty Ltd)

Penguin Books India Pvt Ltd, 11 Community Centre, Panchsheel Park, New Delhi – 110 017, India

Penguin Group (NZ), 67 Apollo Drive, Rosedale, Auckland 0632, New Zealand
(a division of Pearson New Zealand Ltd.)

Penguin Books (South Africa) (Pty) Ltd, 24 Sturdee Avenue, Rosebank, Johannesburg 2196, South Africa

Penguin Books Ltd, Registered Offices: 80 Strand, London WC2R 0RL, England

First published in 2012 by Viking, a division of Penguin Young Readers Group

10   9   8   7   6   5   4   3   2   1

Text copyright © Ann Edwards Cannon, 2012
Illustrations copyright © Lee White, 2012
All rights reserved

LIBRARY OF CONGRESS CATALOGING-IN-PUBLICATION DATA
Cannon, A. E. (Ann Edwards)
Sophie's fish / by A. E. Cannon; illustrated by Lee White.
p. cm.
Summary: Jake starts to worry about everything that could go wrong when he agrees to take care of his
friend Sophie's fish for the weekend.
ISBN 978-0-670-01291-6 (hardcover)
[1. Worry—Fiction. 2. Fishes—Fiction. 3. Humorous stories.] I. White, Lee, ill. II. Title.
PZ7.C17135So 2012
[E]—dc23
2011016227

Manufactured in China
Set in Blockhead and Kennerly

For Rick Walton,
the granddaddy of us all
— A. E. C.

To my students at the
Art Institute of Portland
—L. W.

A GIRL AT SCHOOL named Sophie asked me
to babysit her fish when she goes to stay
at her gram's house this weekend.

"Jake," Sophie said, "will you take care of Yo-Yo?"
I've never met Yo-Yo, but I said okay.
How hard can it be to babysit a fish?

EXCEPT!
Now that I'm waiting for Sophie to bring Yo-Yo to my house, I am very worried.

Very.

I don't know anything
about taking care of fish!

FOR **EXAMPLE!**

What if Yo-Yo gets hungry and wants a snack? What kind of snacks do fish like to eat?

Bug leg Sucker

Strawberry Worm Cake

Bug Wing Sucker

What if Yo-Yo wants to play a game after eating his snack? What kind of games do fish like to play?

What if Yo-Yo gets sleepy after playing games and wants me to read him a naptime story? What kind of stories do fish like to hear?

What if Yo-Yo gets cold while listening to a naptime story and wants me to cover him up with his special blanket? Do fish care if their special blankets are all wet?

Will **I** call Sophie's gram
on the telephone and say,

BUT! What if Sophie's gram doesn't answer? What will Yo-Yo do then? Wait on the front porch for Sophie to come home? And cry?

What do you do with a fish crying
on your front porch?

PLEASE! Tell me quick! Because I really, really need to know! Phew! I'm exhausted! Who knew babysitting fish would be such hard work?

Here's what I think. When Sophie rings my
doorbell, I'll tell her to take Yo-Yo back
home. No fish allowed at this house, I'll say.
This house is a fish-free zone.

Oh no!

It's SOPHIE!

Sophie is right here.

RIGHT NOW!

I open the door.
Sort of.

"Hi!" says Sophie.
"Hi," I say. "Where's Yo-Yo?"
"In his bowl. In my wagon.
Thank you for helping Yo-Yo and me."
Sophie beams at me.
Suddenly I don't feel so worried.
How hard can it be to babysit a fish?

"Feed him twice a day," says Sophie.
"Once in the morning. Once in the
evening."
"That's it?" I say.
"That's it," says Sophie. "Come on.
Let's go get him."
Babysitting Sophie's fish will
be a snap!